caillou

Learns to Swim

Adaptation from the animated series: Sarah Margaret Johanson
Illustrations taken from the animated series and adapted by Eric Sevigny

chouette

The family was spending the day at the pool.
Daddy was already in the water, waiting for Caillou.
"I'm right here, Caillou," Daddy said, holding his arms
open.

The water was deep and dark. Caillou looked around nervously. He could barely see the bottom of the pool. Caillou stuck one foot in the water and shivered.
"Brr," he said.
"Are you coming in, Caillou?" Daddy asked.

Caillou wasn't sure.

"Look, Daddy, it's shiny over there," Caillou said, pointing to the other side of the pool.

When Daddy looked, Caillou ran away to the wading pool where Mommy and Rosie were sitting.

"Whee!" He said, and he jumped in.

Rosie laughed, and Mommy protected her face from the splashing water.

Daddy finished his swim and went over to the wading pool.
"Daddy!" Rosie said.
"Maybe next time you'll come in the big pool with me,"
Daddy said, winking at Caillou.
"Okay," Caillou said, awkwardly.

That night, Mommy tucked Caillou into bed and said,
"Remember the big pool?"
"Ye-e-es?" Caillou answered.
"It was pretty big, wasn't it?" Mommy said.
"I guess so," Caillou said.
"Would you like Daddy to teach you to swim?"
Mommy asked.
"Oh, yes!" Caillou exclaimed.

A few days later, Caillou had his first swimming lesson. He loved being in the water and learning to swim. After just a few lessons, he was less afraid and he was getting better and better.

"Swim over to me, Caillou," Daddy said.

"I can do it," Caillou said.

"I know you can," Daddy said, encouragingly.

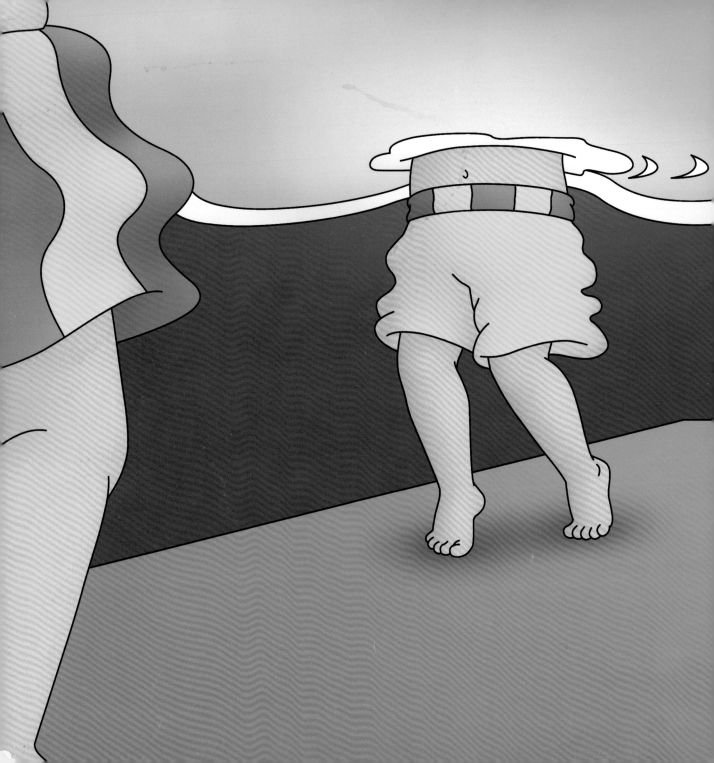

Caillou was still walking a little on the bottom of the pool, but he was moving his arms the right way.

"I'm swimming, Daddy. I'm swimming," Caillou said. He was very excited.

Caillou wanted to swim and dive, just like the big boys and girls.

After a little break, Daddy asked, "Do you want to go back in the water?"

"Yes, I can swim now, Daddy," Caillou said. "Come in and watch me."

He and Daddy got into the pool. Caillou pushed off the bottom and put his arms out and kicked his way towards his daddy.

"That's it. Hold your arms out, just like I showed you," Daddy said.

Caillou walked on the bottom of the pool again, but very soon he was swimming all by himself.

"That's it, Caillou," Daddy said.

"I'm swimming, I'm swimming. See, Daddy?"

"Yes. I'm right here," Daddy said. "Go, Caillou, you can do it."

"Look at me. I'm swimmi- glub glub," Caillou said, splashing wildly.

Suddenly, Caillou was afraid, but his daddy was not
far away.
"It's okay, Caillou. Come this way," Daddy reassured
him. "Take it easy. Swim to me, just like you did before."
Caillou calmed down when he heard his daddy's voice
and swam toward him.

"That was a bit scary, wasn't it?" Daddy said, holding Caillou in his arms. "But you knew I was there, didn't you?"
"Yes, Daddy," Caillou said.
"You know what?" Daddy exclaimed. "You were really swimming all by yourself."
"I was, wasn't I?" Caillou said.
"I'm very proud of you. I knew you could do it!"

©2013 CHOUETTE PUBLISHING (1987) INC. and DHX COOKIE JAR INC.

CAILLOU is a registered trademark of Chouette Publishing (1987) Inc.
DHX MEDIA is a registered trademark of DHX Media Ltd.

Adaptation of text by Sarah Margaret Johanson based on the scenario of the CAILLOU
animated film series produced by DHX Media Inc.
All rights reserved.
Original script written by Matthew Cope.
Original episode #35 Caillou Learns to swim
Illustrations taken from the animated television series and adapted by Eric Sévigny.
Art Director: Monique Dupras

The PBS KIDS logo is a registered mark of PBS and is used with permission.

Chouette Publishing would like to thank the Government of Canada and SODEC
for their financial support.

Books
Tax Credit

Gestion
SODEC

Bibliothèque et Archives nationales du Québec and Library and Archives
Canada cataloguing in publication

Johanson, Sarah Margaret, 1968-
Caillou learns to swim
(Playtime)
To be accompanied by a poster.
For children aged 3 and up.

ISBN 978-2-89718-036-2

1. Swimming - Juvenile literature. I. Sévigny, Éric. II. Title. III. Series: Playtime
(Montréal, Québec).

GV837.6.J63 2013   j797.2'1   C2012-941685-1

Printed in China
10 9 8 7 CHO1983 OCT2016